An Alchemist's Wedding

(a speech on joy and love)

by

KEITH BRAZIL

DEDICATION

To Michael – my Moon Magician

with all the joy and love.

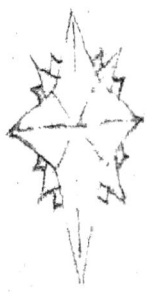

Also, to all the Mad Hatters and March Hares –
Adrian, Ben, Colin, Hendrik, Jason, Mark, Neil, Paul,
Rolf, and Tom – who supported us on our day of
joy, and to everyone on the day for such an amazing
reception and a riotous Pride backdrop.

CONTENTS

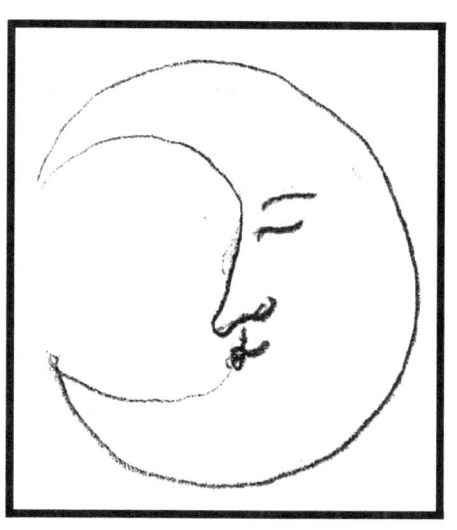

KEITH BRAZIL

ACKNOWLEDGMENTS

Editor: Kitty Malone

Cover Design: Adam Wiltshire

Cover Illustrations & 'The Marriage of Heaven and Hell' Interior Sketches: Michael Brazil

Rose Illustration: Colin Francolino-Scott

Quotes from: Francis Brerat, Kate Bush, The Carpenters, Gloria Gaynor, Joni Mitchell, Rumi, Shakespeare, *Jerry Springer: The Opera*, Sri Nisargadatta, Valum Voltan – Foundation For The Law Of Time.

With special thanks to my wonderful creative team – Michael, Kitty, Adam, Jason, Stephen, and Colin.

A Rose Pink Production.

An Alchemist's Wedding

An Alchemist's Tale of a Chymical Wedding,

a Chimerical Beast,

a Sacred Marriage and the Evolution of Love

through the Gaia 'Heaven-on-Earth' project

or

An Esoteric Astrologer's Delight

(A Moon Ceremony

dedicated to The Magdalena, Bride of Christ)

Also,

An Inconvenient Wedding, Getting There

or

Love Will Find A Way

The Alchemist's wedding speech:

'This is the third time in my life that I have had to stand up and come out; once as a gay man (my business), once on a spiritual platform (Spirit's business), and again now (as both). It allows me to end Descartes's incorrect philosophical assertion, "I think therefore I am" (which could just have easily been "I feel therefore I am" or "I eat therefore I am" or "I am hungry, therefore I eat" or any one of the many zodiacal assertions, or physical, emotional, mental or spiritual aspects we encounter as human beings) by restating that,

"We Are That We Are".

Beyond conception and perception, this speech ultimately becomes a blending of Gloria Gaynor (*I Am What I Am*) meets God (*I Am That I Am*) and she was almost right in that she was what she was (whatever that 'what' might have been!). The theme of my speech today is 'Love, Vision and Encompassing Madness'. It is a two-way test to see if I can get through it without being too emotional and if you can get through it with good humour; I won't be putting bets on either! However, this speech is the serious bit where I need to touch base with the Earth, give out a celebratory transmission message from the other side (it is both a 'passing out' and 'passing in' parade) and explain the extraordinary astrological phenomena occurring at present which has led to this Moon Ceremony and Wedding Celebration – a date intuitively and wisely decided upon by the Magician. So here goes:

Transmission…

Congratulations to the Mad Hatters and the March Hares teams on this day of joy! We have a message to all the lovers and friends, fathers, mothers, sisters and brothers, crystal and rainbow children, magenta masters, barefoot warriors and healers, seers, therapists and therapeuts, missionaries, artists, storytellers, scientists, writers, educators, musicians, carers, communicators, good business men and women, film-makers, managers, journalists, mechanics, designers, BBC-ers, Oxford and Cambridge-ers, disco dancers, philosophers, believers and non-believers, the thinkers, the be-ers and the doers, emissaries of light and ambassadors of the animal kingdoms:

Welcome to the galactic New Millennium! The Earth's clocks are out by 7 years, but the new Universal energy is now active and being applied to the planet as part of a 26,000-year cycle and renewal phase for the solar system. It's a kind of Cosmic Restructuring for our tiny part of the Universe heralding the change for many New Beginnings as we romp towards the magnificent Mayan year of 2012 and 2013 – the end of their calendar and the start of a brand new cycle. The Olympiads will be rewarded as Britannia re-lights her greatness through the celebration of its cultural diversity and unifying acceptance of its differences. She will hold hands with Europa and the Americas. Around the World other land masses and centres of light will re-ignite and re-unite. As a result there will be a series of major planetary shifts for humanity to work through.

At the beginning of 2007 the Beacon of Light for London and the South East of England going into France was spiritually secured and the old earth energy was reactivated and revitalised through the lay lines. Thank you to all of those involved, especially Princess Diana. The harmonious alignment of the planetary beams will last for the next 7 years when, in 2014, a new aspect of universal love will begin the new shaking and bring humanity back into resonance with its Heart centre. As one wonderful planetary wizard reminds us,

"Humanity is the only species in the whole of creation currently living out of sync with Time's universal living cycles, which consequently causes instability within the organic processes and an atrophy of the spiritual senses."

We in Spirit lovingly urge you to reconsider your ways. The spiritual leaders, saints, angels and archangels, goddesses and gods, and nature spirits have been busy building their teams and are now in place to aid humanity to become the responsible adult guardians and protectors of this beautiful, blue-green planet known as Earth. The Sun and the Moon are re-balancing the masculine/feminine principles and Gaia herself is responding, deepening humanity's nurturing principle through the Mother/Child relationship and revealing the true nature of brother and sisterhood. You are the good God earth children. Everyone has a part to play as everyone here is, in one way or another, a pioneer come to work through the transitional energy and help bring in a New Age for the next generation of souls. Some of you will, but some of you won't, be coming back. If you are re-embodying look out for a chance to reincarnate in and around the year 2560 – a special planetary treat and visitation is planned.

The establishment of social living based on spiritual principles has been attempted before in various esoteric experiments. Some here today will remember the courts of Akhenaton, Versailles and other courts of certain Kings and Queens, Emperors and Empresses from around the world, Avalon/Camelot, the Forests of Sherwood, as well as in the Temples of Solomon, and the monasteries and mystery schools throughout history. For various reasons these attempts have often been thwarted. However, the time is now. It is official. The esoteric courts are once again open and this time fully supported by those on both sides of the veil. You are in a position today to fill up this flat with so much love and gladness that it reaches Trafalgar Square and helps light up London.

We send you our love and blessings. Peace and joy be with you on this day of personal, national and international celebration and festival.

Transmission ends…

When helping to organise this special occasion I got into an existential crisis and dispute with the Registrar about what a secular partnership meant.

Having struggled to pull the ceremonial event away from the grips of institutionalised "Churchianity," the State would allow us to use the word love, but not permit reference to God. This made things a little difficult for me, as I wanted the Ceremony to have both a spiritual and creative dimension. Does God recognise marriage certificates or Registrars, for that matter? No, God does not. They, like paper permission, man made morals and matrimony, suffer the same fate as Nietzsche (who, unlike God, is dead) ending up in a philosophical discursive limbo – one of the Creator's sunnier gifts to philosophers!

However, God does recognise and bless souls coming together to entwine lives and combine forces for their onward growth and progression. So, you are now going to get the ceremony and celebration we wanted through sharing, mutual contribution and gift – part of the back-scratching "Bare Necessities" Law of The Jungle – whilst we wait for the social mores, traditions and 'Edicts of Equality' to catch up with the natural spring and fountain that is part of the blossoming and nurturing effect of Love.

So is it to be legality or love, living in sin or common-law status, 'civilisation' or marriage? And what to do if there are children involved? Commitments, energetic partner choices, cherished memories and hopefully not too many regrets – all are to be found within our present-day democratic system. In the words of one female wandering minstrel,

"We don't need no piece of paper from the City Hall, keeping us tied and true…"

This is, in part, a bad Oscar speech, overly long and full of thanks, yet in meeting The Magician I struck alchemical gold and need to acknowledge everyone present (both physically and spiritually) for making it possible. I also need to acknowledge those family and friends who, for different reasons, could not be here today, yet whom we hold dear in our hearts. They too have shared their love and friendship in such ways that have enabled us to be standing here today; so, to family and friends, here and there, old and new, this side and that, the biggest of thank-yous to you all. This wedding could not have got here without all of your kindness, support, generosity, wisdom and infinite patience.

It has been a labour of love, as well as a joy. We would especially like to thank everyone who has contributed to our wonderful day today: our Master of Ceremonies and presiding spiritual Reverend, the hosts, decorators, bus provider, photographers, invite and music makers, caterers, waiters, and, in particular, the groom support teams: the Mad Hatters and March Hares. They are the men of merriment, good cheer and responsibility, heart outlaws, but this time not in tights (although I think some of them would like to be!).

I need to acknowledge everybody, both behind the scenes and in front, as it has been an epic journey to the heartland, of breakthroughs, of recognitions, of evolving expressions of love, of work and the rewards of work: the descent of Grace, further heart opening and joy. Specifically, it was my meeting with The Magician that precipitated in me a new activation of love – an emergence of self and an understanding of The Way ahead. The colourful mosaic that makes up the 'chameleon-I' tries to reflect the best of you and in our meeting it feels as though we have done this so many times before. The Japanese capture it beautifully,

"Two things cannot alter, since Time was, not today. The flowing of water, and Love's strange, sweet way".

Our Way has been guided by spiritual values combining those most volatile of ingredients: love, belief and magic. It is a strange mix, a Wyrdening Way, yet it acts as a catalyst – not only for us but also for the community of friends. It involves the Evolution of Love, the Law at the Soft Heart of the Universe, and the sharing of its many expressions. In physical law, it is evolution in line with Mother Nature. In spiritual law, it is the integrating journey home – the progression of the soul back to Mother-Father God. All things happen by their own nature – God does All, for the sake of just being beautiful. As there is no difference, no separation, between Nature and God as Supernature, the on-going rhythms of Spiritual Science and Poetry-as-Truth continue, and the great Cosmic Dance of planets and molecules is affirmed. Nature not only abhors a vacuum, but inertia as well. In this world motion is everything. The great poet and philosopher Rumi reminds us that,

"Whosoever knoweth the power of the dance dwelleth in God."

Music, song and dance, in their human, physical and emotional forms, with melody and harmony, are important to us; including the blending of the musical forms of the East and West. Not only in spontaneous expression and celebration, but also in their ability to aid the letting go 'of stuff', the working through of issues and in evolving a way ahead. Some of my best ideas have come from the disco floor (a kind of fight through the clatter to the silent and sacred spaces where clarity aids spiritual insight and informs evolving intelligence) – well, that is my excuse for a good night out! Music is particularly important in the formative years where the inner cocoon of self can be explored through the listening to, and establishing of, particularly selected frequencies.

A good regular 'Stomping' and 'Shaking' on the dance floor to free the body, emotions and mind of stuck and difficult energy is, I find, essential. Queen Elizabeth the First enjoyed a good Galliard or two before breakfast. Today on the disco dance floor, that leaves us somewhere between *Let's Dance* and being *Lost in Music* with little or "nothing going on but the rent" (apart from, that is, "the dreams of the everyday housewife…" in this case meaning me, an everyday household yogi and novitiate Alchemist)!

Celebration is, like the symbolic Two Swords, both a dance of Liberation (Freedom) and of Justice – a chance to dance off your chains and re-establish the true self, whether shod or unshod. The Berserkers knew it to violent ends; today it is more of a chance to *Dance Yourself Dizzy* in a juju trance dance of delight. Or, as a certain character from *Jerry Springer: The Opera* declares in an act of spontaneous, anti-authoritarian, body ownership and riotous outburst,

"I just want to fuckin' dance."

So, Mr Heart DJ, keep the soul groove going.

The Magician is my Earth Angel, heart-opener and commune gatherer all in one. He is the link to everyone here. He is the one who enabled this Hermit to finally come down the mountain and put his feet safely on the ground. This tantric joining in love of the instinctual and intuitive, the sexual and the sensual, has led us to this point of partnership and equality: one of the things we as gay men have been fighting for – a sexuality within democracy and a freedom of unrepressed physical expression. The LGBT community of today emerged triumphantly from out of the late blossoming 'queer' sexual revolution; the question remaining – how to integrate our new found social position into a 'progressive spirituality'?

We do not always share the same view point (as many others do not share ours), yet therein lies the rub and necessary point of pressure, friction and heat for the relationship processes to develop. Please be kind to any over-spilling mistakes in the experiment and expression of our alchemy. In the re-written words of the immortal Bard,

"If we have offended, think on this, and all is mended…"

However, we do expect tolerance of differences, and more positively, acceptance and appreciation – for that is what Love is.

Slowly, through honest negotiation and deeper understanding, we are learning new ways of intimacy and relating. It is a work-in-progress, but has been such a fertile relationship, full of growth and development, of growing up and growing down, of cats, kittens, crystals and gardens, of cooking, art and conversations, of great fun and great pain, not only of Love's pleasure, but also its darkness, of renewal through magic, love and childlike joy. In parts it was The Mysterious Case of Inversely Reciprocal Cinderellas: one stuck at the ball and one stuck at the work surface never getting to the ball. Yet, as everyone knows, a well-balanced pair of balls means we can all have a blast! As that wonderful song of The Carpenters goes,

"I'm on the top of the world lookin' down on creation and the only explanation I can find is the love that I've found ever since you've been around..."

The last 3 years saw the final deep centrifugal spin of the Buddhist Cross in an effort to remove the unwanted and unnecessary stuff of the past age that cannot evolve: such things as selfishness and materialism, polluting and despoiling, control and indoctrination. Those things not in line with the Natural Way of Faith and Love cannot go forward and need to be dismantled. This is our individual personal work as we each tend to our gardens – the removal of weeds, as well as enhancing the Heart's blooming.

Whether seen as Karma and/or the stuff of our childhoods, it was necessary to bring deep wounding and confusions to the surface so that sexual and spiritual healing could be completed. The worm was brought out of the wood and treated, the dry rot cut out so the new wood, blossom and wassailing could begin. It was also necessary to get us up to the right speed and frequency for the harmonious energy being applied to the Earth through the new planetary alignment for the next 7 years. We must respond with Gaia for we all now have a chance to "dance our dreams with our body on". They will be memorable years – make them so.

The mad spin cycle was also necessary to allow us to establish new ways of being, to explore and self-pattern within the inherent chaos. We worked diligently on learning to un-judge. It pointed the way to the ending of suffering and the choosing of personal happiness. It also showed us the true nature of sacrifice – the surrendering of old pain, attachments and ways of behaving. In an initiatory soul drama the chimerical beast of darkness, desire, ignorance, and wrath was fought. Yet these un-transmuted passions and elements that help make up matter and the challenge of adversity hold all the secrets of soul ascension and love. We find that in muck, if utilised wisely, is a kind of magic.

One dear friend summed the whole Karmic/ cause and effect thing up in a wonderful saying,

"Mon ami. We have an expression in France. Unless you have a clean plate, don't throw merde up in de air as it will land on ze face".

How fabulous!

Yet out of the negative grows the positive leading to the healing of divisions and the development of New Ways. Of this we are learning. There is no perfect plan, only the finding and sharing of 'A Way'. In this civil partnership we are beginning a conscious path of "combining forces", slowly and cautiously or quickly and whole-heartedly, depending on whom you are with. There is a truth in each of our opposites (although I am mainly right – ultimate proof of how wrong I am!).

Anyhow, we will continue to shuffle along in our own little/big shambolic, yet convivial, musical theatre way. With The Magician's poor sight and my terrible hearing it will continue to be a kind of strange, soft-hard, shoe-shuffling comedy double act, lost characters from the somewhat entertaining 'Mr and Mrs' show, but which one is which? In the end it matters not, for "this old shoe met his old sock".

It has been an Alchemist's marriage, which involves not knowing that it is until after the event, as no one would consciously opt for it, but pre-supposes a belief in an active, creative, Divine Intelligence running through the Universe. It is a kind of applied, practical, and sustainable chemistry for human hearts mixed by the Great Alchemist in the Sky.

Our particular Over Seer of operations stirring our spiritual pot is the ancient aboriginal Goddess Una – Earth Birth-Mother – who entwines our Dreamtime. We are certainly in the stew as she sprinkles just enough drama and spice to our lives to create soul food for the Cosmos. As we dissolve back into the elements that make up the Fabric of Existence we know as Life, we are also absorbed back into the Shiva-Shakti marriage of Truth and Love – both the beginning and the end of All-things.

For anyone following their heart it is a spiritual journey, but an Alchemist's tale involves star-crossed lovers, shadow partnerships, twins, 'twixt and betweens', mirrors, parallel dramas and group stories. Some of the players are conscious and others not, but all play an essential part in the name of Love and Renewal, not only for the people involved, but for the earth energies of the planet. For some it is a surrendering to, and acceptance of, fate, destiny and higher will through the yearning for it. To others it is a daily Buddhist's choice of electing and, through the choosing, and hopefully of their highest choice, the growth and development that results.

Thus fate and free will, destiny and choice, interlink and lead to the discovery of creative joy through the celebration of love subject only to the vagaries of God, Dame Fortune and the incredible physical forces of Nature. So unto them we must surrender: our lives merely being a small merciful part of their Divine Unfolding Plan and Whim. We thank Mother-Father God for their tenderness.

When I met The Magician, through mutual friends in a bar, it was love at first sight. It took all of three seconds and I fell into a film, an all-singing/all-dancing 'zom-rom-com'. He has enthusiasm and love in abundance, yet he is also unfocused, uncontainable, and a law unto himself as he follows his impulsive moon dreams of happiness. Yet, for all The Magician-mess I have found myself in, he has brought me so much joy.

The testimony to this is in his smile, which looks very much like the Cheshire Cat or a new moon grinning down at you in India amidst the playful Ganges in the foothills of the Himalayas. It is also found in his expressive face and eyes that I have found myself endlessly looking into, as well as within his characterful, theatrical form. He gets to hum "tiddly-pom" and I get to sing a line from one of my favourite songs,

"Hey there Michael. D'ya really love me?"

The Magician proves time and time again that, yes, he really does. For One with so many loves in his life I am lucky enough to be his bloke, his fella, and have been blessed with what the Chinese would call "a slow-burning passion", although I think The Magician wishes it was somewhat faster and more enthusiastic! Yet that is just The Magician wanting me to be more like him whereas I am in it for the epic long haul of exploration and exchange (probably me wanting him to be more like me). Whichever, I am sure we will be exploring some unresolved father/son issues and divergent points of view along the way!

Magician, I love you. You are my Ganesha, my bear, my partner in crime, my friend, my Buddhist monk, and my boundless, energetic dancing partner. You love me like growly thunder and, in doing so, draw subtlety from me. It is perplexing. At best I love you as the peaceful rain descending (refreshing and fertile, rather than soggy and depressing); at worst as the conjuror of storms and the volatile "hurricane that comes for you". Yet in reality, I am only a defensive, spiky puffer-fish and an exasperated nag-hag from Hell insistent on knocking the nonsense out of you… although, at times, so in love with all your fluff and stuff.

We have been together four years, more of a wisteria entanglement than an engagement as we were thrown together so quickly. It feels we have been married several times, including a special ring ceremony given within a circle of stone one Winter solstice at Avesbury. Thank you guys (you know who) for taking us down there and helping to make our commitment day so special. That time has enabled us to deepen our understanding of each other's behaviour, particularly those patterns of expressing hurt and anger.

More importantly, we learnt how to ask for each other's help (once our dominant would-be sergeant-majors, tyrants and bossy bullies, as well as our subjugated victims, saints and martyrs, were put to one side, that is!). We both continue to shine a light into our dark spaces, dispelling myths and fears until we find the smiles of our friendly faces once more, however long it takes to behold our inner beauty and peculiar truths.

This understanding of the guiding principles behind our relationship enables us to lay the foundations of the next phase of love and work together as we are now in conscious possession of the spiritual laws and sub-laws in operation – all emitting from a central source of Divine Love. The Magician is particularly interested in developing and deepening the use of the 33rd degree and sub-law of

Unconditional Love – the Way of the Pink Compassionate Heart (of which he already has his Masters and is showing us The Way). That is why he presents you with a rose quartz heart today, whilst I offer you the gold bubbles of champagne. Catch them on your nose and tongue if you can! Love is, after all, a celebration of the many senses.

As part of this partnership we are still discussing the joining of names. The former name (informally adopted) of 'the Cheshire-Darlings' has been cherished, but might simply be amended to 'the 'Lovelys'. This would be a great surname for us both to adopt as people could enquire,

"Where have you been?"

"Oh! I've been to tea with the Lovelys".

That would be much easier to spell and sign than any complicated, hyphenated surname, but unfortunately it has been rejected by The Magician because, he says,

"We're not all living in a children's story."

Hmph!

As it is a Capricorn full moon (of initiation) in Cancer, Ruler of the Moon, we are going to call upon Mary, The Magdalena, working through the Goat Star of Gladness, Capella, to connect us all in a Moon Ceremony. This will help us, like George in *It's A Wonderful Life*, to lasso the moon, anchoring it to the Earth as joy within our hearts.

It is written that our moon might be the last our planet has and holds secrets yet to be revealed. Balancer of gravitational forces, part creator of earth life, the night and the seasons, controller of growth and governance of waters are some of the known qualities of the Moon, yet that Mystic Orb also holds newly discovered, yet very old, elements (Helium 3, for example). Esoterically, it houses part of the secret of the 13th astrological sign of the lunar cycle, Arachne, and the occult mystery of the feminine and the Goddess. It also holds a secret of synthesis and of the only colour to be found on the moon – orange, and the gift of ginger.

The Moon is such a precious gift to our planetary system; we must cherish it and wed it to the Earth.

We must consciously keep it safe in orbit and not push it away from us. It is also a chance for us to re-dress the balance of the importance of the Lunar to the Solar masculine and to honour the intuitive feminine. So, as part of our partnership ceremony I am going to lead you through a brief ribbon-binding, wool weaving and moon ceremony entitled: Glisten!

For all you non-believers just try to be open minded and think of connecting to everyone here in love. If anyone wishes to knit a bedspread for Bosnia afterwards you are most welcome!'

Moon Ceremony & Prayer/Dedication & Vows

Before you all here on this day

I do declare my solemn intention to you Magician that:

I will give my love to you freely and forever

I will be your guide and take your guidance through life's journey

I will respect your choices and support your endeavours

For richer, for poorer, in sickness and in health

Till my mortal body fades and I return to life as spirit.

All: To this union all here have witnessed. May you stand together united, in love, forever.

(The Kiss!)

Reading: *Love Poem* by Rumi

First Dance: *I'm in Heaven/Dancing Cheek to Cheek*

Honeymoon: India/Paris.

Serenade: *On the Street Where You Live*

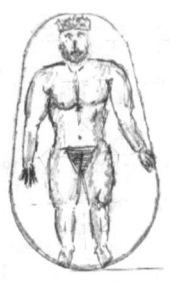

ABOUT THE AUTHOR

Keith Brazil was born in Broadstairs, Kent, England. He trained in Dance Theatre at Laban Trinity Conservatoire, London, and was a founder member of 'Adventures In Motion Pictures' Dance Company. He has worked as a freelance professional dancer, choreographer, teacher, and dance lecturer. Keith has also trained as a Complementary Therapist in Spiritual Healing and Reflexology. He gained a degree in English Studies and is currently engaged in writing a collection of metaphysical and fictional stories, essays, poetry and novels. His first book The Wilderness Diary was published in December 2012. In Consideration of Cats and Popcorn, Parasites, Precious & Pearls were published in Autumn 2013. The Chameleon's Last Dance was published in 2014. Keith lives in London with his partner Michael.

www.ingramcontent.com/pod-product-compliance
Lightning Source LLC
Chambersburg PA
CBHW050918120626
46552CB00004B/1639